A SMALL FIRE

A SMALL FIRE
POEMS BY RUSSELL KESLER

Pecan Grove Press San Antonio, Texas

ISBN: 1-931247-01-3

Pecan Grove Press
Box AL
1 Camino Santa Maria
San Antonio, Texas 78228-8607

Acknowledgments

Thanks to the editors of the following journals, in which earlier versions of some of the poems first appeared.

Art Speak: "That Day"; *Black Dirt:* "Wednesday Morning"; *Chariton Review:* "New Research Indicates that the Fetus Dreams"; *Chili Verde Review:* "Ants and Moth" and "Song of the Open Hand"; *Connecticut Review:* "Shrimping in the Indian River," "From a Fifties Childhood," and "Bluefish"; *English Journal:* "Habanero" and "Jonah, Later"; *The Florida Review:* "Elegy" and "Mr. and Mrs."; *Grasslands Review:* "Sighting by the St. Johns"; *Isle:* "Fiction," "Gnatcatcher," and "Harvestman"; *The Marjorie Kinnan Rawlings Journal of Florida Literature:* "After a Line by Su Tung po," "Kingfisher" and "Where Do Birds Go to Die?"; *Negative Capability:* "Skinning Squirrels"; *New Virginia Review:* "The Barn" and "Self Portrait"; *The Olympia Review:* "Locked Out," "Mockingbirds," "Sunday" and "Walking"; *Paintbrush:* "His Picture" and "Love Letter"; *Quarterly West:* "Waking at Night"; *Southern Humanities Review:* "July" and "Pileated Woodpecker"; *Southern Poetry Review:* "Screech Owl at Two A.M."; *Sou'wester:* "Cat, Cardinal, Dusk," "The One Born Blind," A Small Fire," and "Snakebird"; *Wilderness:* "Blackbirds"; *Willow Springs:* "On the Bus"; *Zone Three:* "Returning"

"Blackbirds" also appeared in the anthology *Wild Song: Poems of the Natural World,* The University Press of Georgia, 1998. "July," Kingfisher" and "Song of the Open Hand" also appeared in the anthology *The Orlando Group and Friends*, Arbiter Press, 2000.

I am grateful to Judith Hemschemeyer and Don Stap for their responses to many of these poems. And thanks to Phil Deaver, Terry Hays, Pat James, Susan Lilley, Jeanne Schubert, and Terry Thaxton for counsel and friendship.

for Martha

CONTENTS

I. SATURN THROUGH BINOCULARS

The Barn / 15
Skinning Squirrels / 16
From A Fifties Childhood / 17
Cause And Effect / 18
A Small Fire / 19
That Day / 20
Some Answers I Didn't Offer My Son / 21
On The Bus / 22
Saturn Through Binoculars / 23
The Lesson For Today / 24
Mason In The Cemetery / 25
The Last Drive-In / 26
Floaters / 27
Self Portrait / 28
Love Will Be Spoken / 29
Undertow / 30
Elegy / 31
Mr. And Mrs. / 32

II. LOCKED OUT

Returning / 35
Mockingbirds / 36
Sunday / 37
Gifts / 38
Walking / 39
His Picture / 40
At The Clothesline / 41
Love Letter / 42
At The Window / 43
Waking At Night / 44

Stray Dog / 45
Locked Out / 46

III. *Ants and Moth*

Cat, Cardinal, Dusk / 49
After A Line By Su Tung-Po / 50
Fiction / 51
Pileated Woodpecker / 52
New Research Indicates That The Fetus Dreams / 53
Ants And Moth / 54
Habanero / 55
Sighting By The St. Johns / 56
Farmer's Wife Turns Hubby Into Scarecrow / 57
Where Do Birds Go To Die? / 58
July / 59
Jonah, Later / 60
Blackbirds / 61
Screech Owl At Two A.M. / 62
Snakebird / 63
Trimming The Muscadines / 64
Bluefish / 65
Shrimping In The Indian River / 66
Root Canal / 67
Kingfisher / 68
Song Of The Open Hand / 69
Wednesday Morning / 70
Harvestman / 71
Gnatcatcher / 72
The One Born Blind / 73

Life is a pure flame, and we live by an invisible sun within us. A small fire suffices for life.
                    —Sir Thomas Browne, *Urn Burial*

I SATURN THROUGH BINOCULARS

THE BARN

Chestnut walls shoulder twilight,
banked to the rafters in kudzu,
breasting the sinuous rush of August corn
that tides around them.

Swifts dip to skim the caving roof,
ladling their trebled chatter into blue air,
and I look for Pap's square stoop to emerge,
the mules watered and stalled,
his last chore the arcing climb to the house
where my father will be born.

A plow teeters in a corner,
upright from old habit.

But it is too quiet;
something is listening that cannot hear me.
Dust sifts from the ridgepole's cracked heart.

The moon is fast on the corn,
the wind's long sweep pulling.

SKINNING SQUIRRELS

A shallow slice middle of the back
left a pouch large enough for two fingers,
and Granddad and I leaned away
from each other over each warm carcass,
slow peel of hide uncovering the sack
of membrane and muscle. Then he'd hack through tail
and neck, elbow and ankle, and slit
the length of the belly, pass the entrails
to the patient dogs. That easily—a sharp knife,
our hands opposed in work with one intent—
the silver pelt reversed like socks pulled off
in haste. I sometimes closed my eyes, the blood
and smell of tripes too much for me. He'd laugh.
Young squirrel was good meat, meat was life.

FROM A FIFTIES CHILDHOOD

The noon whistle started with a groan
and rose to a howl.

Dogs rolled out of sleep
to stretch and bark at shadows.

Some people sat to ham and cherry pies,
some drew up to cornbread and cold greens.

The whistle sat atop the water tower
where the town's name shimmered in the sun.

The sound filled every street and house.
The time was noon, the day was every day.

CAUSE AND EFFECT

Because the neighborhood drunk
drifted over the curb, splintered the post,
a bright new mailbox bakes in June sun.

He pulled up, sheepish,
as I tamped the last shovel of dirt,
offered a twenty, which I took.

But not before I purpled my thumb
with a hammer too big for the job,
burned a hole in my nail

with a glowing paper clip to let
the hot blood flow. It felt so good
I thanked the drunk. I thanked the hammer

and hoisted the new red flag.

A Small Fire

The table laid simply,
the first camellias brimming a bowl
between us, buttered toast
and a grapefruit halved
our mid-winter plenty;

the Gulf has lent a mizzle
that is blearing the windows,
but light fills this room,

a small fire,
the grapefruit husks pocked
like the full moon
that set unseen as we woke.

THAT DAY

The day the car rolled over Neal
she threw out the clothes he'd been wearing,
new corduroy jumper and striped shirt.
This was after the race to the hospital,
after she knew he'd live, his back bearing
the mark of the tread like white dirt.

When she lifted him off the gravel drive
a mewling cry bled from his lips
like the first sound he made at birth.
Twice he'd been given to her alive,
kicking and taking the air in sips,
delivered, this time, from the hard crust of earth.

SOME ANSWERS I DIDN'T OFFER MY SON

The man on the bench at the bus stop
holding his head
in both hard hands
mourns for a life lost,

wife and children a line of dust
on a long, straight road,
the brother he never knew,
the father he did know,

or he's wrecked after a night
with a fifth of busthead,

or he's just discovered that, though
an old friend invited him
for a hot meal,
hot bath, warm bed,
he spent the bus fare on the call,

or weeps for joy at breath,
or nothing at all.

ON THE BUS

The skinny redhead harnessed to his walkman
grins as if he has the answer.
A waitress tells the driver all her troubles,
the blind man knows his stop and rings the bell.

I try to read, but I'm drawn to the scroll
of landscape beyond the scratched glass,
scraps of street and dark houses,
a boy setting bags of garbage by the curb.

I imagine a life I might have led,
there, where lights are going on,
a curtain slowly being drawn.
For now we have a destination.
The driver turns the big black wheel.

SATURN THROUGH BINOCULARS

Someone told me that you could distinguish
the rings and fabulous colors
but all I can make out between
intersecting tree limbs
is a shining orb gone soft
around its edges
like a streetlight seen through tears.

A planet dances in the glass
like a paramecium.
To hold it steady in the sky
I lower the binoculars,
regard the thing as Job would have done
while his boils simmered and the stink
of his dead flocks migrated toward heaven.

THE LESSON FOR TODAY

Mason sits in his car and listens
to the Haydn waltz his son is learning,
the piano faint, the teacher clapping time.

He remembers his own hands fumbling
on the keys, Mrs. Tiller immense
beside him, how her moist eyes bulged
behind her glasses, the airless little room
smelling of menthol. She had a daughter,
he recalls, pretty, who people said was wild.
She spoke to him once, and sometimes
she confused his dreams, her red lips
forming words that left him when he woke.

Now he watches his son's lamplit profile intent
above the keyboard, the woman beside him counting.

MASON IN THE CEMETERY

Mason rides his son's twelve-speed for exercise
through azalea-scented neighborhoods,
the citrus also heavy on the air.

He rides through the cemetery, where it's quiet,
no traffic growling behind him, huge oaks
dusting the asphalt with blossoms. It's spring,
but he's thinking about summer, long gray
and yellow afternoons, when from the graveyard's
highest hill he'll watch storms build above
the city he knows so well, and why
this offers solace he can't imagine.

One granite stone he passes represents
a tree trunk broken off, and he pedals faster,
cliché closing in from all sides.

THE LAST DRIVE-IN

For years the cracked marquee read CLO ED, and chains
were looped across the IN and OUT. Now the screen's
a pile of broken cinder block. Humped rows
of grass resemble trench works he's seen
at Fredricksburg and Shiloh. The speakers lean
at baffled angles, and Mason knows

this show is over. The one-eyed caretaker
roamed the moonlit aisles, and a night returns
when a girl with blond hair on her arms
cried into her hands against the door.

Now only the concession stand remains,
and on its roof the whitewashed booth that beamed
the story out across the quiet field.

FLOATERS

Lately, when Mason reads, a question mark
trails the words across the page. And sometimes
when he's looking at the sky, a phantom hawk
tilts and wheels through the clouds.

The doctor he consulted called them floaters,
said they're just another subtle sign of aging.
Mason left by a different door
and couldn't find his car.

Now he sees the subtle signs everywhere,
hair curling from an old friend's ears,
a dream in which he's being chased by question marks.
It's nothing, he tells himself, but nothing works.

FOUR FOR JIM BALLEW, 1944-1987

Self Portrait

You hold a largemouth bass
close to the camera,
the skin on its back dark as deep water,
your face still full and tanned.

I imagine you composing the shot,
setting the stop and speed, the timer,
lifting the fish from its bed of damp towels
so the red gills flare.

What the picture doesn't show
is how you waded out knee-deep
and released it, watching until
it moved away from blinding light and air,
the great mouth working as if in speech.

Love Will Be Spoken

The day we reshingled your kitchen roof
you wouldn't stay in bed,
mounting the ladder at noon
with sandwiches and cold beer,
the fever you never shook
bright in your eyes.

Mary was afraid you'd fall.
I wanted to tell you
the task itself was thanks enough.

But love will be spoken,
and you chanced the gabled slope
with both hands full.

Undertow

The account of a stranger's death,
how he entered the surf
to save a friend
and was swept away,
brought back your face
in that narrow bed,
flushed with fever,
struggling above the sheets
like that swimmer's in the foam,
tugged out of reach
while we stood on level ground
and watched you go.

Elegy

Because the live oaks hold
their long argument with gravity,
pegging heavy limbs out
parallel with the horizon,
they come to earth gracefully,

as you did,
touching down more than once
before settling in the grass,
still reaching,
still singing with the wind.

MR. AND MRS.

Across the fence and the wind
he told me about the last day,
how she shivered and didn't open her eyes
when he touched her,
fifty years that far gone.
While we talked, a mockingbird began
a filigree of song,
counterpoint gone off the deep end
of dusk, naming the stars
as they broke out and bulked around us.

Tonight, through a half-curtained window,
I see his hand reach into lamplight,
perfect in desire,
and I think of your hands, their strength,
each fine bone nestled
in its own meaning.

II LOCKED OUT

RETURNING

The night I had the stroke I lay twelve hours
on the floor, unable to reach the phone
beside the bed. I struggled, at first,
against my body's weight, but then deep peace
came over me. I prayed and slept, I dreamed
my way through years. My sons were boys again,
I rode that thrumming tractor, and once
Marie caressed me in my sleep. At eight
that morning, Jim, my youngest, found me;
he said he'd let the phone ring twenty times.
I knew then what the music was I'd heard,
and when Jim asked me how I felt, I knew
the words I needed were beyond us,
receding as this life pulled me back in.

MOCKINGBIRDS

A pair of mockingbirds has built a nest
in the white camellia by the kitchen door.
The neighbor's cat will lurk, a moon-eyed tabby,
but when I shoo him off they rail at me.
I see their point—they own the earth in ways
we lumbering walkers never will.
They dive at me each time I use that door.
And sometimes, late at night, one chants and sings,
as if to challenge silence or make light
of something we can't understand. I lie awake
and listen to that song, more beautiful
because it has no melody, no pattern.
The old hymns make me weep, but that voice raised
against the darkness takes me through the night.

SUNDAY

Today the sermon came from *Lamentations,*
reminding us of Jeremiah's folly
in questioning the plans of a loving God.
I listened for a while. Self pity
is a devil I have come to know too well.
Outside, white clouds tugged shadows to the east
and a flock of crows rowed hard into the wind.
The preacher's voice made poor accompaniment
to that shifting light and shade, majestic
silence, and a moment came when something
broke inside me, a lust I haven't known
for years. It's hard to see this as a sin,
desiring more of pain and pleasure,
lamenting what we lose in gaining heaven.

GIFTS

While learning to feed myself again
I ate a lot of soup. For weeks my shirts
were spotted with my supper. The nurse
was patient—she tied the bib for me—
but I refused to be spoon-fed. Now I'm back
to knife and fork fare—chicken, chops, the food
my father said a man should eat. Advice
was rare around that house, but he did tell me
this: "Keep plugging. One day you'll wake and find
that you have everything you wish for."
And I do. Or did. Some things are lost
and hard work earned some back. Not Dad's hands, though,
the rough nails caked with clay. Not Mother's voice,
not yet, calling *Lewis, come to supper.*

WALKING

This afternoon at four I took a walk,
the first since the stroke. I shouldn't say
I walked, it's more a stutter-step, right foot
leading. The cane helps some, but it's all new
to me, the weight in my left leg, the way
the pavement tips and rocks beneath me.
Alone on the street, I stopped to watch
a thrasher work the duff beneath an oak,
and tasted some sweet pollen in my throat.
I'm blessed by my long life. I know that.
But while I watched, that bird picked up a twig
and left the earth so easily a leaf
beneath its wing was all that moved. I cried
then, and nothing's come to tell me why.

His Picture

In crayon on white paper, my grandson
drew a picture: sky with birds, two round trees,
and me, foregrounded, one hand raised in greeting.
He's put in all he knows of me, the cane
I'm leaning on, felt hat, a spot of red—
peppermints—outside one pocket. The sun shines
in his picture, but I don't throw a shadow.
I'm merely there, as permanent as grass
and trees and light. He's signed his masterpiece
beneath my feet in alternating strokes
of blue and red. Allan. He's eight, blond hair
going brown. His love for me is larger
than the two of us. When ragged speech came back
after the stroke, his name rolled off my tongue.

AT THE CLOTHESLINE

My knees are stiff, my fingers ache, the clothespins
squeak in humid morning air. Eight o'clock,
and anvil clouds crowd the horizon
in the west. The clothes begin to steam
before I've stretched them on the line, the first
cicadas start their daylong drone. Yesterday
it stormed at two. I woke from a dream
in time to watch the sheets sag in the grass,
speckled with new mud. I love to watch
a thunderstorm becoming what it is
out of nothing more than heat and water.
Its time is short, but it gives back to earth
what it has taken. These summer mornings,
the spirit of the rain is rising.

LOVE LETTER

Bill Hooks came by today, Marie, to help me
pick the grapefruit. Despite the freeze last Christmas,
the tree was sagging under its great load.
We struggled with the ladder, told jokes,
drew blood on thorns and twigs. And though we filled
two croaker sacks, we didn't take it all.
From the kitchen window, our job half-done
looks finished now to me, rich green below,
the top half lit by lamps of yellow fruit.
If you were here you'd fret about the waste,
you'd call the boys to come and pick the rest.
But love, you're gone for good, gone for good.
And it seems right to let this bounty hang there,
kissed by rain and wind until it falls.

At the Window

The blue jays at the feeder scold the squirrel
who seems to feel the seed is there for him.
When I put the feeder on a pole
he climbed it. When I hung it from a chain
he clung by his back paws and gorged himself.
I tried a plastic owl that frightened
everything but him. The next-door neighbor
says I'll never win. "The only thing to do,"
he said, "is put him in a Brunswick stew."
He laughed, and I let it pass. I know
that squirrel from any other. One ear
is nicked, he's fat, his fur is glossy.
It's early August. The acorns are bitter,
and holly berries won't be ripe for months.

WAKING AT NIGHT

The farm in Indiana still returns
in dreams so bright they often wake me.
Marie and I are standing in the yard
beneath the great black cherry she so loved.
I try to talk with her but every time
she speaks, a hard wind out of nowhere
takes her words. Yet all the common sounds,
the Hereford yearlings bawling in the barn,
the feeder covers banging in the lot,
come through above it all. At last she turns
and walks back to the house. The kitchen door
slaps shut behind her, and I turn to face
the numbers on the clock beside the bed,
the ringing silence not yet charmed by birds.

STRAY DOG

Today a stray dog followed on my walk.
I've seen him in the neighborhood,
nosing garbage cans, his neck and head
a sullen curve. But his company
was welcome. He heeled as if we'd walked
that way for years, and when I stopped to rest
he sat and waited, leaning on my leg.
I don't know why he chose today to join me,
or why, halfway home, he growled, barked once
and bolted, his long nails gouging the asphalt.
At home I found his yellow hairs clinging
to my pants, and his sour breath stayed with me.
I burned my supper and left the pan outside,
poor offering for a hunger I can't touch.

LOCKED OUT

Some days I think I've mostly lost my mind.
Twice this week I've locked the keys inside
and had to struggle through the bedroom window.
The second time I had to laugh, and wondered
what the neighbors would have thought—an old man
breaking into his own house, or maybe
sneaking out. More and more, I find that laughter
helps me through these days, though sometimes I
discover I've forgotten why I'm laughing.
Most things are plain enough—the laundry
piles up, my stomach complains, I cross off
yesterday first thing each morning. The clock
my mother gave us chimes the hours.
One day, I know, I'll forget to wake.

III *Ants and Moth*

CAT, CARDINAL, DUSK

A single note tweaked
in a twilit azalea
is all it takes to free her
from dog-worry, or the spell
of small, warm hands.

She's all for the hunt,
pupils big as blueberries,
mincing paws testing each purchase
for yield and snap.

In this game she's back
in some tangled covert
she remembers without knowing,
and this bird is the last chance
before snow licks her shadow clean.

But her inch-and-crouch method presumes camouflage,
and her gray and white pattern
is a moving shadow in a windless hour.

The cardinal is matching his song
to her motion,
informing his ground-hugging mate
of her progress
with ascendant notes
that answer the brightening stars.

AFTER A LINE BY SU TUNG-PO

Boatmen and waterbirds dream the same dream.

Boatmen and waterbirds dream the same dream.
Slow water rolls between banks of black mud
carrying goldfish and stars on the stream

of night. As galaxies bend light, a gleam
inside the heron's brain unfolds a flood
of hunger for the river's one dream.

The boatman sighs and turns, the caulked beam
that carried him upriver his dry bed.
He thinks he hears goldfish and stars stream

beneath the bow. His sleep's a braided seam
he follows down the current toward some god.
Boatmen and waterbirds dream the same dream,

know cicadas' songs by heart, know the name
the river gives all things, even lilypads
and goldfish silted by the stars that stream

across the eyelid of the sky. Thick as cream,
the river scours rock, its water warm as blood,
while boatmen and waterbirds dream a blue dream
of goldfish and stars borne away on the stream.

FICTION

Anywhere the squirrel turns
the dogwood's bright berries burn
within reach. Low sun picks out
the lichens on the limbs. No doubt

a story's waiting here. A hawk
might slash into the scene, all beak
and talons. A twig this rodent
trusts could break. But the moment

passes, uncomplicated
by development. The red
fruit vanishes, black paws drop flakes
of bark like snow. No one's heart aches.

PILEATED WOODPECKER

He carries his mad whinny
through every room in the woods.
Ordained to dig,
he's still a craftsman
and eyes his work closely.

Symmetry is his passion,
the fist-size rectangle,
his tattoo on a pine
ripe with grubs.
When he looks at his wife
he sees himself.

In the joinery of his dreams
he planes fragrant planks of walnut,
feathers the floor of his nest
with white oak,

dovetails boxes so perfect
his laughter cannot escape.

NEW RESEARCH INDICATES THAT THE FETUS DREAMS

How much we need to know about our kind,
including what the fetus has in mind.

Since tests can measure REM in one so young
and inexperienced in thought and tongue,

let's test the sperm and egg while they're discrete
to see if dreams are possible in gametes.

Then focus tighter, on napping atoms,
whose slumber might suggest important data

that take us farther inward. What nightmares
might awake when we can ride the light years

back to dreams of what it's like to be
before blood and breath begin to ask for me.

ANTS AND MOTH

A line of ants emerged from a crack
behind a light switch in the kitchen.
Individuals ventured off the track
but never far. I followed that thin
column across tile steppes and grout valleys
around the stainless sink's rim to a moth
they were dismantling. Wings lopped, antennae
relaxed and crossed, it lay in a cold broth
of coffee. But this is no elegy
for moths, littering the windowsills,
dusting the walls, all that energy
trying to swallow the light that kills
them anyway. More beautiful the ants,
glistening on sweet morsels in their trance.

HABANERO

One bite, and your world
has changed. This isn't
the first sip of scalding coffee,
or steam on knuckles
above the uncovered pan,
but heat that drives the tongue
to silence, heat
the coldest water
cannot soothe.

And you cry, knowing
you asked for it,
nourished the plant,
admired the wrinkled globe's
thrift and color,
consumed it,
weighing the grace
of flavor
against the promise
of fire.

SIGHTING BY THE ST. JOHNS

It took four lanes
in three low surges
brown under the pink tongue of morning,
then was gone
in a hole it opened
in the roadside weeds.

Panther, moving north
with the coiling river
into miles of grass,
leaving a print slowly filling
with dark water.

If I'd been looking
in the rearview
I'd have missed it, perhaps
noticed the sedge quivering
and driven on.

But I was watching
the river mist over the road,
ready for the shadow
that rose and disappeared,
lean ghost with light at its heels.

Farmer's Wife Turns Hubby
Into Scarecrow

He came in with the barnyard on his boots
and swung at her because supper was late.
When her head hit the stove she saw black stars
and from that moment started praying.
Every night she willed her dream to work on him.

One day he said his head felt empty
as a gourd. She held her tongue, somehow.
The hair on his forearms was going blond.

The morning he didn't come to breakfast
she found him in his bed gone stiff and light
as a dime store dummy. His hair was hay,
his eyebrows grass two days after frost.
Most wonderful of all, his eyes were blank as pot lids.

She took him to the garden, staked him up
between the cabbage and the corn.
The crows flash their black wings above his head.
She tells people that he just got tired of her.

WHERE DO BIRDS GO TO DIE?

How often do you see a dead bluejay
or a mockingbird heels-up in the back yard?
Sure, sometimes the cat gets lucky,
and you might see a sharpshin nail a robin
in mid-air. But what happens
to the thrasher whose heart stops
on an oak limb ten feet above the driveway?
Think how many crows have loitered over,
dusk and dawn. A feather might drift down
to lodge in summer grass and though
you search the sky, that bird is gone.

JULY

Changing its perch in the dogwood,
a cardinal stirs faint thunder
among the pendant leaves.

A fist of cumulus rises
over Green Swamp, cicadas string
their chains of silence in the oak.

For one moment, the yard
is hushed and still, poised
as if for some important truth.

Then a line of invective
from the thunderhead,
a distant chain saw kicks in,

and the cardinal moves once more
in its small storm of need.

JONAH, LATER

I remember the heat, the briny stink
of shrimp and weeds, slick walls of muscle flexing
in the dark. And often in my dreams
I hear the eerie moans and calls, distant
like a shofar down the desert wind,
then so near they seem to thrum inside me,
prayers in a voice I didn't know I had.

Puddles everywhere, gurglings that echoed
the sailors' babble when the lot came to me,
the wind through the rigging as the mast snapped.
When it was over and I walked the streets
of Nineveh, I stopped at every well
to taste sweet water, turned my face up
to the sun to let my tears burn dry.

BLACKBIRDS

For two weeks now, their wheezing treetop patter
has been a kind of daytime serenade,
music lacking melody and matter.
Their whistling and clucking, those notes played
by hinges gone ungreased so long they squeal
when forced ajar, are anything but song.
They're up there by the hundreds. What appeal
bids them congregate? Is their need to throng
so great that blathering is no disgrace
and the solitary voice should have no say?
It's doubtful conversation's taking place.
But something does get said. Every day
near dusk, with one mind their black clouds rise,
leaving silence empty as their yellow eyes.

SCREECH OWL AT TWO A.M.

Sometimes at dusk they swoop on the cat,
beaks clicking, no sound from wings swollen
by the press of air. They swing from the live oak
to the cherry's scrawl and back, until the cat skulks off
behind the house. I've seen a flying squirrel
plucked from flight and borne squeaking
to the darkness under the ilex.

Just now, when I woke hearing that mournful trill,
I thought one of the children was crying,
bending the sobs as when they're sick
or a bad dream stands shrouded at the foot of the bed.
But it's an owl alone under the white moon,
facing nothing but a still, clear night,
singing for something to do.

SNAKEBIRD

Slicing the surface for air,
the S of neck and head trails a slick
instead of ripples, and cruises,
disembodied, like a fable come alive.

In the crazed light off the lake
a bream glints in its beak,
then the flash of that patented toss
to take the fish head-first,
its shape descending in the bird's throat.

Anhinga when it glides at hawk-height,
darter when it flies beneath the surface,
but snakebird parting water and air.

On a cypress branch it's water turkey
unfolding its wings to dry, a magician's cape
to trap the afternoon sun.

TRIMMING THE MUSCADINES

In March the vines began to stir,
traveling through blue days
when returning warblers stopped to rest,
then under knives of summer lightning
becoming familiar with rain warm as buckshot
and the clamp of the noon sun.

Asking nothing, they accomplished
the thick-skinned fruit and shade
so deep it muted bird call.

Now, when I cut them back,
unraveling their slow, stubborn miles,
though it's February each stub brims
a clear drop that will glaze
to meet frost for a while.

BLUEFISH

The bluefish is so full of himself
he cranks his steel jaw shut on the shank
of the hook. His flanks are firm, oiled
by mucus. Cold water has trimmed him.

The voltage of his surge made the line sing
in the guides. When I pulled him from the surf
a fingerling mullet clogged his throat.
These teeth are honed for slashing, the flat

yellow eye never closes. Goodness
and mercy aren't part of the plan.
I'll lay him open, peel back the skin.
Salt water has rendered his flesh sweet.

SHRIMPING IN THE INDIAN RIVER

Shrimp are strong swimmers,
so move the net slowly.
If you stab at them,
they squirt around the rim
like trails of mercury.
Full moon plays big in this,
and the kerosene lanterns
that pull them to the surface.

It's as quiet as that moment
when the choir has sat down
and the preacher stands there,
gathering his words.

Only the riffle of the current
around the anchor line,
emptying Mosquito Lagoon,
and the nets dripping moonlight,
filling the buckets
with what the river has to give.

Root Canal

While he reamed with his abrasive needles
the endodontist hummed to himself.
He might have been walking the dog,
or shopping for wine.

I could see my molar
in his glasses, the hole he'd opened
in its crown to expose
the recalcitrant nerve.

"Not much blood in there," he said
behind his mask. "This
should have been done a long time ago."
He was doing all the talking
but I thought I knew
what he meant.

A fat white cloud crossed the window
and, good patient that I am,
I took that for a sign
that having one less nerve
might be a good thing.

KINGFISHER

His voice rattles in his throat
and he needs a haircut,
but he knows how to nail himself
to the sky, hovering above the river
while minnows mingle and flash
inside his eyes.

He thinks living well means taking all he needs,
claiming any dead branch
to consider the plume of hatchlings
dreaming against the current
and the ripples he'll leave
when he plunges.

If he leads with his chin,
if his blue head is too big and his beak
a spike, he's punching holes in the mirror,
he knows what's behind the clouds.

SONG OF THE OPEN HAND

Thank you for the live oak's rough bark,
for the way it tore my skin today
to remind me, while I worked,
that I am blood and water.

I've decided to thank you for something
every day, not because I have so much
but because I want more—long days, green lives—
and that tells me I'm here.

When I open my hands I find an X
in each palm. I don't know what that means,
but if I press them together
I can't carry anything. Tomorrow,
I'll thank you for that.

WEDNESDAY MORNING

Someone is running
even now
running for her life
for the life of the baby
slack in her arms
her black skin gleaming
feet bare on the stony road

This is far from here
far from my red chair
from the words the pencil leaves
on the page
fine black lines
I can cross out
the a the e the o

HARVESTMAN

No web for daddy-long-legs,
no geometry spangled with dew.
Lurking in a corner will do.
The hunkered, pinhead body begs

belief that there's room for eyes,
guts, mouth, brain. And what about sex?
He has eight narrow knees to flex.
Still, the nonchalant crouch belies

the speed he's capable of.
He thinks of his work as conquest,
rather than kill. As for the rest—
the gore, the small cries—it's only love.

GNATCATCHER

Below a ragged line of crows
the smallest bird in sight,
a gnatcatcher on a bare crepe myrtle,
bends the green reed of his song.

He has no crest, no mask
to make his face mysterious
and beautiful. He's a slip
of blue and gray, a patch
of morning sky on lichened bark,
and I'm the one watching him.

THE ONE BORN BLIND
—*John 9.6-7*

When the one born blind
had washed the clay from his eyes,
he could see the wind
move through the olive grove,
and the gloss on the raven's back.

How the clouds must have amazed him,
his sunburned fingers cupping
the bowl of coins,
his face in his wife's black eyes.

And at dusk, his back to a palm
still warm with sun,
he could watch heat lightning quiver
behind the rocky, cropped hills,
weary from so much seeing,
wondering if sleep would be darkness
he could wake from.

Alyn, Glen. *Huckleberry Minh: a walk through dreamland*. 1999.
    ISBN: 1-877603-61-9 $15
Browne, Jenny. *Glass*. 2000.
    ISBN: 1-877603-69-4 $7
Byrne, Edward. *East of Omaha*. 1998.
    ISBN: 1-877603-44-9 $12
Frost, Helen. *Why Darkness Seems So Light*. 1998.
    ISBN: 1-877603-58-9 $12
Gotera, Vince. *Dragonfly*. 1994.
    ISBN: 1-877603-25-2 $8
Hall, H. Palmer, ed. *Radio! Radio!* 2000.
    ISBN: 1-877603-70-8 $7
Harper, Cynthia J. *Snow in South Texas*. 2000 (Reprint).
    ISBN: 1-877603-26-0 $7
Hoggard, James. *Medea in Taos*. 2000.
    ISBN: 1-877603-66-x $12
Kennelly, Laura. *A Certain Attitude*. 1995.
    ISBN: 1-877603-28-7 $10
Knorr, Jeff. *Standing Up to the Day*. 1999.
    ISBN: 1-877603-65-1 $12
McFarland, Ron. *The Hemingway Poems*. 2000.
    ISBN: 1-877603-74-0 $7
McVay, Gwen. *This Natural History*. 1997.
    ISBN: 1-877603-45-7 $7
Mulkey, Rick. *Before the Age of Reason*. 1998.
    ISBN: 1-877603-60-0 $10
Oughton, John. *Counting Out the Millennium*. 1996.
    ISBN: 1-877603-37-6 $10
Radasci, Geri. *Ancient Music*. 2000. ISBN:
    1-877603-67-8 $7
Reposa, Carol Coffee. *The Green Room*. 1999.
    ISBN: 1-877603-59-7 $7
Rodriguez, Michael. *Humidity Moon*. 1998.
    ISBN: 1-877603-54-6 $15
Scrimgeour, J. D. *Spin Moves*. 2001.
    ISBN: 1-877603-71-6 $8
Seale, Jan Epron. *The Yin of It*, 2000.
    ISBN: 1-877603-68-6 $6
Teichmann, Sandra Gail. *Slow Mud*. 1998.
    ISBN: 1-877603-55-4 $10
Treviño-Benavides, Frances. *Mama & Other Tragedies*. 1999.
    ISBN: 1-877603-63-5 $8
Van Cleave, Ryan G. *Say Hello*. 2001.
    ISBN: 1-877603-72-4 $12
Van Riper, Craig. *Convenient Danger*. 2000.
    ISBN: 1-877603-62-7 $7

Forthcoming from Pecan Grove Press: Books by Kathryn Kirkpatrick, Edward Byrne, Dan Stryk, Ingrid Wendt, James Cervantes, Patricia Valdata and John Gilgun